When Willy Went to the Wedding

Written and illustrated by Judith Kerr

PictureLions
An Imprint of HarperCollins*Publishers*

~ For my husband Tom ~

First published in hardback in Great Britain by
William Collins Sons and Co Ltd in 1972
Reprinted in 1994. First published in Picture Lions in 1977
New edition first published in 1994
10 9 8 7 6 5 4 3 2
Picture Lions is an imprint of the Children's Division,
part of HarperCollins Publishers Limited

A CIP catalogue record for this title is available from the British Library.

ISBN: 0 00 195906 9 (HB) ISBN: 0 00 661340 3 (PB)
The HarperCollins website address is: WWW.fireandwater.com.
Printed and bound in Singapore

Once there was a boy called Willy.
He had lots of pets and a grown-up sister.
Willy's sister was so grown-up
that she was getting married,
and Willy was going to the wedding.
"Shall I bring my pets to the wedding?" said Willy.

“No,” said Willy’s father.

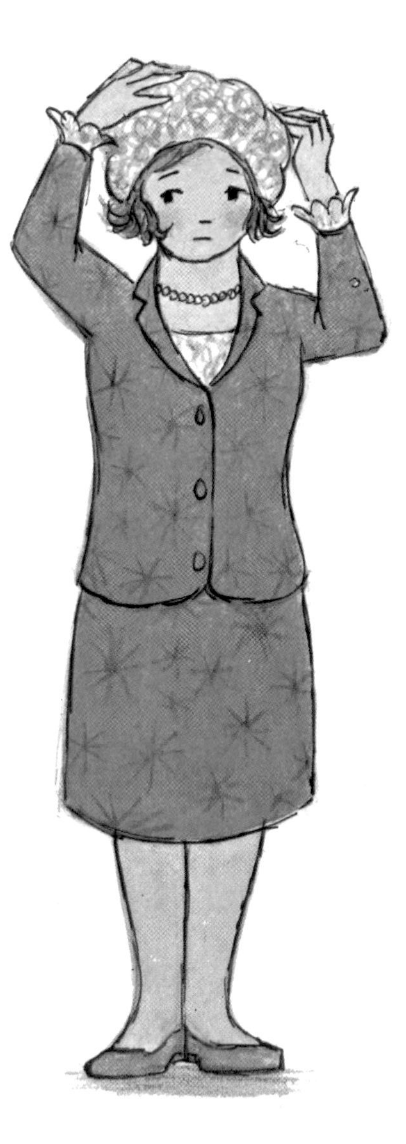

“No,” said Willy’s mother.

“No,” said Willy’s grown-up sister.

“Better not, old chap,” said Bruce, who was going to marry Willy’s sister. “Your pets might not like it.”

So Willy did not bring his dog to the wedding.
He did not bring his cat or her three kittens.
He did not even bring his goldfish.
He only brought his hamster
because it liked to be in his pocket,
and his frog so that it would not be lonely.

"Come on!" cried Willy's father.
"Everyone is waiting at the church."
It was not far.
"Remember to walk slowly,"
said Willy's father.
"And remember to
hold up my dress,"
said Willy's sister.

The church was full of friends and uncles and aunts.
They all turned to look at the bride.
"I think I'll take a picture of the wedding,"
said Willy's Uncle Fred.
Suddenly one of the aunts screamed.

"Look!" she cried.
It was not Willy's fault that his cat
had followed him to church.
It was not his fault that the three
kittens had followed the cat.

"Cats don't come to weddings," said the vicar.
Willy said, "I'll look after them."
The vicar gave them something to sit on.
Then he married Willy's sister to Bruce.

"Now for the wedding picture!"
cried Willy's Uncle Fred.
Everyone stood quite still.
But Uncle Fred did not stand still.
It was not Willy's fault that his
dog was waiting outside the church.
It was not his fault that the dog
was pleased to see him.

"How disgraceful!" screamed Willy's aunt.
"Take your pets home!" cried Willy's mother.
"At once!" cried Willy's father.
"I think they'd be happier there, old chap," said Bruce.

There was food and drink for everyone at home.
Willy said, “I’ll give my pets something to eat.”
The hamster was hungry too.

"Now I will take my picture of the wedding,"
said Uncle Fred.
But Willy's aunt screamed.
"A mouse!" she screamed.
"A horrible orange mouse!"

It was not Willy's fault that his hamster was hungry.
It was not his fault that the hamster liked cake.
And it was not Willy's fault that his frog wanted a drink...

...or that his aunt was frightened of frogs...

...or that the cats got all upset.

None of it was his fault,
but everyone was cross.

“Take your pets away!”
cried his mother.
“Right away!”
cried his father.
“Away! Away! Away!”
screamed his aunt.

“But what about the picture?” said Willy.
“What about the picture of the wedding?
My pets should be in it.
After all they did all come.”

"No!" cried Willy's mother and Willy's father.
"No! No! No! No! No!" screamed Willy's aunt.
Uncle Fred set up his camera.
"I'd better go then," said Willy.
But Bruce said, "Stop!"
Willy stopped.
"I don't agree at all,"
said Bruce.
"I am very fond of pets
and I should love some
in my wedding picture."

"Just a moment!" said Willy.
He ran to get something.

Uncle Fred clicked his camera.
It was a lovely wedding picture.

“I’m glad my goldfish
wasn’t left out,” said Willy.
“Even a goldfish can enjoy
a wedding.”